A NORTH-SOUTH PAPERBACK

Critical praise for

On the Road with Poppa Whopper

"Poppa Whopper and his daughter, Frannie, are free spirits whose road adventure begins when a man announces that their house must be torn down by noon. A minicamper with bathtub on top becomes their home as they try new jobs each day. De Beer's quirky artwork, which pictures their various jobs—as cookie testers, housepainters, pig rescuers, and artists—catches the simple spirit and strong affection of the pair. With short, good-humored chapters and syntax and vocabulary that aren't too demanding, this chapter book is lots of fun." *Booklist*

On the Road with Poppa Whopper

er

First published in Switzerland under the title *Papa Wapper und das rote Wohnmobil*

First published in the United States, Great Britain, Canada,
Australia, and New Zealand in 1995 by North-South Books,
an imprint of Nord-Süd Verlag AG, Gossau Zürich, Switzerland.
First paperback edition published in 1997.

Library of Congress Cataloging-in-Publication Data
Busser, Marianne.
[Papa Wapper und das rote Wohnmobile. English]
On the Road with PoppaWhopper / by Marianne Busser and Ron Schröder ; illustrated
by Hans de Beer ; translated by J. Alison James.
Summary: After their house is torn down, Frannie and Poppa Whopper
transform a rusty old van into their new home and travel around the
countryside earning their living doing an assortment of odd jobs.
[1. Fathers and daughters—Fiction. 2. Occupations—Fiction.]
I. Schröder, Ron. II. De Beer, Hans. ill. III. James, J. Alison. IV. Title.
PZ7.B9665Pap 1995 [Fic]—dc20 94-40890

A CIP catalogue record for this book is available from The British Library.
ISBN 1-55858-373-4 (trade binding)
1 3 5 7 9 TB 10 8 6 4 2
ISBN 1-55858-374-2 (library binding)
1 3 5 7 9 LB 10 8 6 4 2
ISBN 1-55858-776-4 (paperback)
1 3 5 7 9 PB 10 8 6 4 2
Printed in Belgium

For more information about our books, and the authors and artists
who create them, visit our web site: http://www.northsouth.com

Contents

Opportunity Knocks Only Once!

One fine morning a workman knocked on the front door of Poppa Whopper's house.

"Do you live here?" he asked.

"Yes," said Poppa Whopper. "Nice, isn't it?"

"It was nice," said the man. "Unfortunately it's got to go. The house must be torn down."

"What?" said Poppa Whopper. "Then where would we live?"

"How should I know?" said the workman. "My job is to tear the house down, not find you a place to live. I have my orders from the mayor's office."

He showed Poppa Whopper an official paper.

Frannie came to the door. “What does he want, Poppa?” she asked her father.

"He wants to tear down the house," explained Poppa.

"But that is crazy," said Frannie.

"Now, you listen here," the man said to Frannie. "By twelve noon this house has to be flattened to the ground. There is nothing I can do about it."

"You mean *today*?" asked Poppa Whopper.

"That's right," said the workman. "The construction company comes in this afternoon to start work on the new town hall.

"Poppa," asked Frannie in a whisper. "Is this what all those letters were about that you kept throwing away?"

"Could be," said Poppa. "Could be." Then he sighed. "Well, we'd better start packing."

"But Poppa!" cried Frannie.

"That is the only thing we can do," said Poppa.

Poppa and Frannie carried everything outside: the refrigerator, the sofa, the washing machine, even Poppa's tools.

"What are we going to do now?" asked Frannie sadly. All their things were in a big pile on the lawn.

"We should look on this as an opportunity," said Poppa Whopper. "Time to move on, to try something new."

"Wait," said the man. "I have an idea. My cousin has a little red van for sale. Wouldn't that do? Why not take a look?"

"Not a bad idea," said Poppa.

And off they went.

The Rusty Little Caravan

The van was battered and rusty.

"It's so sweet," said Frannie.

"You like it?" asked Poppa Whopper.

"It's great!" cried Frannie, delighted.

"She's right," said the salesman. "It can go forwards and backwards. And with a little luck, it'll even take the curves."

"Not bad." Poppa Whopper whistled through his teeth.

"All that for one ninety-nine," said the salesman, beaming. "And I'll throw the wheels in for free—even a spare!"

"That is only fair," said Poppa Whopper.

"You said it. You'll never see a deal like this again," said the salesman.

"Is that right? Well then, I'll take it."

"I wish you the best of luck," said the salesman. "Would you like a bag?"

"No, thanks," said Poppa Whopper. "We'll take it as is."

Off they drove, by fits and starts, back to the house. Or back to where the house used to be . . .

"Finished already?" asked Poppa Whopper.

"Of course," said the workman proudly. "It went down like a house of cards."

"And where are all our things?" asked Frannie, when she saw the heap that used to be their house.

"Don't panic," said the man. "Everything is over there, on the grass, all clean and tidy."

"Good," said Poppa Whopper. "Then we'll organize our new house-van."

"Poppa! It's not a house-van. It's a *caravan*, like the Gypsies!" said Frannie.

"Would you like some help?" asked the workman.

"Sure," said Poppa. "But don't break anything!"

Together they built a bunk bed in the back, sawed a hole for a window, and hung up the cupboards and their best paintings. Slowly it started to look like home.

"Where do you want the bathtub?" asked the workman.

"On the roof, of course," said Poppa Whopper. "Next to the washing machine."

Then they were finished.

"Have a good trip!" cried the workman. "It looks splendid!"

"We're on the road!" Frannie called out of the window. Poppa Whopper started up the caravan, and away they went.

Engine Trouble

"So where are we going to go?" asked Frannie.

"I have no idea," said Poppa Whopper as he turned onto the highway.

"Hey, listen to the engine. It sounds like it's sneezing."

Tch-ch-ch-eeroo, went the engine.

"Bless you," said Poppa Whopper.

And then they stopped.

"I think it's broken," said Frannie.

"Could be," said Poppa.

"Should I phone for help?"

"Good idea," said Poppa. "I'll push it to the side of the road."

When the mechanic arrived, he took a look at the engine and sighed.

"Well?" asked Poppa Whopper.

"It's had it," said the mechanic.

"Is it ruined?" asked Frannie.

"That's what I meant," said the man.

"But how can we go anywhere?" asked Frannie.

"Hmm," said the man. Then he grinned. "You could hitch up a horse to your van."

"We don't have a horse," said Poppa.

"This kind of car should never be sold without a horse," said the man.

"We have a spare wheel," said Frannie helpfully.

"That won't do much," said the man. "It needs a spare engine."

"Do you have an engine with you?" asked Poppa Whopper.

"Well, of course, my car has an engine, but . . ."

"Then we'll take that one," said Poppa Whopper cheerfully. "That is the solution. I'll give you a hand with it." And he took his tools to the mechanic's car and set to work.

"Well," said Poppa Whopper. "It's out."

"Your engine is out too," said the mechanic.

"Then we can swap," said Poppa Whopper.

Together they lugged the engine from the mechanic's car to the caravan.

"Tighten the bolts and it will run like clockwork," said the mechanic.

"I'll give it a try," said Poppa Whopper.

Rrrr . . . rrr . . . rrrrrrrr! went the engine.

"It's running!" cried Frannie.

"It is a great engine," said the mechanic. "But there's only one problem. What am I supposed to do now?"

"Don't you have a horse with you?" asked Frannie.

The man shook his head.

"It doesn't matter!" cried Poppa Whopper. "We'll tow you to the garage."

"If you're sure you don't mind," said the mechanic, relieved.

The Cat-Wash

"We haven't got any money left," said Frannie.

"How is that possible?" asked Poppa Whopper.

"I don't know, but the money is all gone."

"Then we'll have to get jobs," said Poppa. "Without money we can't even buy bread."

"This is really serious," sighed Frannie.

Poppa thought for a moment. "Is there any soap left?"

"Yes," said Frannie.

"Good. Then we can start a cat-wash."

"A what?" asked Frannie.

"A cat-wash. Go up on the roof and run a bath. With lots of bubbles! I'll find our first customer."

Poppa Whopper spotted a kind-looking woman. "Good morning," he called. "Do you have a cat, by any chance?"

"Yes. His name is Felix," said the woman, smiling.

"Well, today is your lucky day!" said Poppa Whopper. "Because we are cat washers. We'll wash your cat until he looks as good as new."

"Oh, how wonderful," said the woman. "I'll go and get him."

"I can see already," said Poppa, "that Felix is in desperate need of a good wash." He handed the cat to Frannie. "Dip him in the bathtub, please," he said.

At last Felix was clean. They dried him off and handed him back to his owner. "Here you are," Poppa Whopper said. "As we promised, good as new." The woman paid Poppa and gave her clean cat a kiss.

“He even smells fresh,” said the woman. “Thank you!”

“It was our pleasure,” said Poppa Whopper, and he drove off to the next house.

“This is great!” cried Frannie a few hours later. “We’ve already washed fifty-two cats.”

"One more and then we'll quit," said Poppa Whopper. "Or we won't have any soap left for me. Just look at how dirty I am!"

"If I were you, I'd just jump in the bathtub," said Frannie.

So Poppa Whopper got into the bathtub, head first, without even taking off his clothes. But that didn't matter, because his clothes needed a good wash too.

And after him, it was Frannie's turn.

In the Cookie Factory

"What time is it?" asked Poppa Whopper one morning.

"Almost ten o'clock," said Frannie.

"Time for a cup of coffee," said Poppa.

"We don't have any more coffee," said Frannie. "The cookies are gone too, and we're out of money again."

"We just passed a cookie factory," Poppa said. "I'm sure we could get coffee and cookies there."

"How?" asked Frannie.

"You just watch," said Poppa, turning the van around.

"Good morning," said Poppa Whopper. "I am the new cookie tester."

"What did you say you are?" asked the manager of the cookie factory.

"Cookie tester," repeated Poppa. "These days there is one in every cookie factory. You don't want to sell bad cookies, now, do you?"

"But my cookies are not bad," said the manager.

"Have you had them tested?" asked Poppa Whopper.

"Oh, well," stammered the man. "Of course not."

"Then how can you be sure?" asked Poppa Whopper. "Have you baked any today?"

"Yes, of course. Honey cookies, butter cookies, chocolate chip cookies, and macaroons."

"We have our job cut out for us," said Poppa Whopper. "We'd better get started."

"Certainly," said the manager. "Do you need anything else?"

"A cup of coffee, please," said Poppa Whopper. "And a lemonade for my assistant."

"Coming right up," said the manager.

"We'll get right to work," said Poppa Whopper.

Frannie tried a chocolate chip cookie, and Poppa Whopper started with a honey cookie.

"Well?" asked the manager anxiously. "Do they pass the test?"

"Hard to say," said Poppa Whopper. "I can't really be sure until after the sixth one."

He took a bite out of the seventh honey cookie.

"Is it good?" asked the manager.

"Rich and delicious," said Poppa Whopper. "Just one more cookie and we'll be on our way. With this job, I can't work for too long or I get a stomachache."

"I can understand," said the manager.

"Well then," said Poppa Whopper. "Here's our bill for the tasting. I'd appreciate it if you could pay in cash."

"I'm very grateful to you," said the manager, handing him the money. "I feel so much better knowing our cookies passed the taste test."

Bean Sausages

A few hours later Poppa Whopper pulled up in front of a butcher's shop.

"May I help you?" asked the butcher.

"We're looking for work," said Poppa Whopper.

"What luck," said the butcher. "I could use some help. Can you make sausages?"

"Who knows," said Frannie. "We certainly enjoy eating them."

"You can start right away," said the butcher, smiling. "Here's the pig." He pushed a huge pig into the workroom.

"What are we supposed to do with a pig?" asked Frannie.

"Well, make sausages, of course," said the butcher. "I'll come back and check on how you are doing." And then he went back to the front of the shop.

"Did he really mean that?" asked Frannie.

"I'm afraid so," said Poppa.

"But that's *horrible*!"

"Don't worry," said Poppa. "I'll think of something."

"Grunt, grunt," said the pig.

"Quiet," said Frannie. "Poppa is thinking."

"I have an idea," said Poppa Whopper. "First we'll hide old Curly Tail in the cupboard."

Then Poppa Whopper ran as fast as he could to the grocery shop and bought fifty cans of kidney beans. He ran back, opened all the cans, and gave them to Frannie. Frannie emptied the beans into a bowl and mashed them up. Then Poppa added spices and spooned the beans into sausage casings.

"Splendid sausages," Poppa said, satisfied.

"But what are we going to do with the pig?" asked Frannie.

"Patience," whispered Poppa. "You go and get the butcher. I'll get rid of the cans."

"These are wonderful!" said the butcher. "They're so good, I'll pay you double."

He paid them and went right back to the shop to sell his fresh sausages.

"Time to move on, Curly Tail," said Poppa, laughing, as he opened the cupboard door. "It's okay, you can come out now. We are taking you to the zoo."

And that is just what they did.

"Sit still up there," Frannie called out. "Or you'll tip over the bathtub."

And Curly Tail sat quite still, because he was overjoyed at not being made into little sausages.

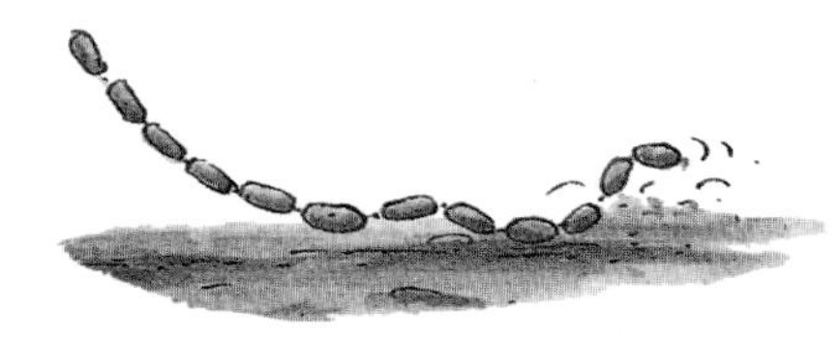

A Letter to the Queen

"What shall we do today?" asked Frannie when Poppa Whopper pulled up at the post office.

"Let's deliver the mail!" Poppa Whopper suggested.

"Do you have any mail left to deliver?" asked Poppa.

"Yes indeed," answered the postmaster. "Three whole sacks left."

"Hand it over," said Poppa, "and we'll deliver it."

"Are you postal workers?" asked the postmaster.

"Today we are," said Poppa Whopper.

He carried the mail bags to the caravan.

"So," said Poppa. "The first thing we have to do is sort the mail."

They sorted the mail into neat stacks: a pile of letters, a pile of postcards and

a pile of magazines and newspapers.

"Hey, look at this!" Frannie said. "This letter is open."

"Letters are private," said Poppa. "Just seal it, quickly."

"But the letter is for the queen!"

"Oh ho," said Poppa. "Now that is something else. It could be vitally important. Go ahead, read it aloud."

Frannie started: “Kärä . . . rä Dr . . . ott.”

“Stop kidding!” cried Poppa.

“But that’s just what it says,” said Frannie. “See for yourself.”

“Well, I’ll be a monkey’s uncle,” murmured Poppa. “It really does say that. I wonder where the letter came from . . . let me see. Oh, of course, it is a letter from Uppsala.”

“Is that far away?” asked Frannie.

“Very far,” said Poppa. “Let’s take this letter to the castle right away.”

Luckily the queen happened to be at home.

"Oh, how lovely," she cried. "I have been waiting all week for that letter. You see, I entered a competition, and that letter tells me whether I won or not. Let me see!" She read the letter.

"Well?" asked Frannie.

"Oh," sighed the queen. "What a shame. I came in sixth. Oh well, next time it might go better." She looked up from the letter. "What a sweet little caravan," she said. "Do you really live in it?"

"We certainly do," said Poppa. "It's our home sweet home."

"Now, that is simply enchanting," cried the queen, and she invited them in for a cup of tea.

An Artist Is Born

The next day Poppa Whopper and Frannie passed a paint store. Out in front, in a pile of rubbish, there was a box filled with old cans of paint.

Poppa Whopper stopped the caravan. "Are they empty?" he asked.

"There's some paint left in all of them," said Frannie.

"Let's take them, then," said Poppa Whopper. "Today we become painters."

"Great!" cried Frannie. "But what will we paint?"

"Houses," said Poppa.

They drove along street with big houses. "There!" said Poppa. "That house certainly needs to be painted."

He rang the bell. "Good morning," he said. "We would like to paint your house."

"That would be wonderful," said the lady.

"How should we paint it?" Frannie asked.

"Oh, I'll leave that up to you," the lady said. "You're the professionals."

"Very good," said Poppa Whopper. "Then we'll get started right away."

They painted the house red, and green, and blue, and purple. And orange and brown and pink. It was quite beautiful.

"Finished!" cried Frannie.

"Me too," said Poppa Whopper; he wiped his brow. "Phew! That was hard work."

The lady came outside to take a look at her freshly painted house.

"This is HOR-RI-BLE!" she screamed. "My house looks like a patchwork quilt. This is a mess! An eyesore!"

"What did we do wrong?" asked Frannie.

"I don't know," Poppa Whopper said. "They were very good paints."

"A mess! An eyesore!" scolded the woman.

Just then a large car pulled up in front of the house. "Oh dear!" cried the woman. "Here comes my husband! What will he say?"

A man as round as a balloon got out of the car. "Wow!" he said, smiling. "It is spectacular. This house must be worth a million now. It's not a house, it's a work of art!"

"You mean you like it?" asked the woman.

"Oh, darling," said the man to his wife. "It was a brilliant idea. I'm speechless." He turned to Poppa Whopper. "Would you like to paint my car, as well?"

"If you'd like," said Poppa Whopper, astonished.

"I think it would be fantastic!" cried the man. "Trust me—I'll make you rich and famous throughout the world."

"I don't know about that," said Poppa, laughing.

A Real Whopper

The round man took them to his factory.

"You can paint anything here. Bicycles, lamp shades, teaspoons, anything," said the round man. "Leave it to me, and soon everyone will have a real Whopper in their house."

"What's a Whopper?" asked Frannie.

"Something that you two have painted," said the man.

"Wow, that's great!" cried Frannie.

"It is unique," said the man. "It is art!"

He got them paints and brushes. "To work, people. Tonight we'll be rich!"

"All right, then. Off to work," said Poppa Whopper.

He took a wastepaper basket from the shelf and began to paint as fast as he could.

The man was thrilled. "I'll go and get more paints and brushes," he said.

Poppa and Frannie had a lot to do. They painted one wastepaper basket after another. Then they painted bicycles, pitchforks, tablecloths, bunk beds, and toasters.

“I’ll take these over to the shop,” said the man. He stuffed his car full of the painted things and drove off. In half an hour he was back.

“I’ve sold everything!” he cried. “Everyone wants a Whopper!”

“But we’re getting awfully tired of painting,” Poppa said with a sigh.

“Oh well,” said the man. “Being an artist isn’t easy.”

"A little more blue and this lamp will be finished," said Frannie.

"Good!" said the man. "And then quickly do the next one. I can easily sell a hundred of these."

"No. Enough is enough," said Poppa Whopper. "We have finished painting."

"But don't you want to get rich?"

"I already am rich," said Poppa Whopper. "I have Frannie. Every day we have something to eat, and we live in the prettiest little caravan in the entire world. We're taking the afternoon off. Tomorrow we might come back and paint some more. If we feel like it."

"If it's got to be, it's got to be," said the man, grumbling. Then he smiled. "I'll just call them Limited Edition Whoppers. They'll be even more valuable!"

"Hurray!" cried Frannie. "What are we going to do now?" she asked her father.

"Whatever you want," Poppa said.

"Then let's go out to eat pancakes."

"Good idea," said Poppa.

Two Gold Medals

"Get up!" Frannie cried. "Someone's knocking at the door."

"Ignore it," said Poppa Whopper in his sleep. "It must be a mistake."

Bang. Bang. Bang.

"I'll just go and check," said Frannie. She jumped out of bed and opened the back door of the caravan. "Hello!" she said to the round man.

"You are famous!" called out the man. "It's in the paper. You have been called the best painters in the entire country!"

Poppa yawned. "I don't want to paint anymore. No umbrellas, no radios, no tents. Nothing!"

"You don't have to paint," said the man. "But don't you want your prize?"

"Prize?" said Poppa, and he rolled out of bed in slow motion. "When will we get this prize?"

"In fifteen minutes, in front of the palace!"

Poppa jumped to his feet. "Then we have to hurry!" he said.

The queen ran to the door and opened it wide. "It gives me great pleasure to present you with this prize," she cried. She had two great golden medals in her hand.

"Allow me," she said. "One for you, and one for you."

"Thank you very much," said Poppa. "But we're fed up with art. We're giving up. We're moving on. We want to be on the road again."

"I understand," said the queen. Then she asked, "And where will you go now?"

"Just drive around and see the countryside," said Frannie.

"Oh," cried the queen. "Could I possibly come along? I absolutely adore your little caravan."

"No problem," said Poppa Whopper.

"Could I sit in the bathtub while you drive?" asked the queen.

"Only if you wear a seat belt!" said Poppa, and he started the engine.

All the people stood and waved to Poppa Whopper and Frannie and the queen as they drove off in the little caravan. Poppa Whopper said to Frannie, "We're living like royalty, aren't we?"

"We are, Poppa," she said with a laugh. "We certainly are."

HB-11-92

About the Authors

Marianne Busser and **Ron Schröder** were both born in the Netherlands. Ron works for Dutch television, and Marianne writes articles for newspapers and magazines. One day they started to write together: children's stories and songs for magazines, for radio programs, and for television shows like *Sesame Street.* They live together with their three daughters, Anne, Jette, and Liselotje, in the Netherlands. Liselotje is still a baby, but Anne and Jette can already read a little—and this book is going to be right at the front of their bookshelf.

About the Illustrator

Hans de Beer was born in 1957 in Muiden, a small town near Amsterdam, in the Netherlands. He began to draw when he went to school, mostly when the lessons got too boring. In college he studied history, but he was drawing so many pictures during the lectures that he decided to become an artist. He went on to study illustration at the Rietveld Academy of Art in Amsterdam.

Hans de Beer's first book, *Little Polar Bear*, is very popular around the world. The book has been published in 18 languages. Hans had so much fun illustrating it that he did more and more picture books. He likes to draw polar bears, cats, walruses, elephants, and moles.

His books have received many prizes, among them the first prize from an international jury of children in Bologna, Italy.

Hans de Beer now lives in Amsterdam with his wife, who is also a children's book illustrator.

NORTH-SOUTH EASY-TO-READ BOOKS

Rinaldo, the Sly Fox
by Ursel Scheffler, illustrated by Iskender Gider

The Return of Rinaldo, the Sly Fox
by Ursel Scheffler, illustrated by Iskender Gider

Loretta and the Little Fairy
by Gerda Marie Scheidl, illustrated by Christa Unzner-Fischer

Little Polar Bear and the Brave Little Hare
by Hans de Beer

Where's Molly?
by Uli Waas

The Extraordinary Adventures of an Ordinary Hat
by Wolfram Hänel, illustrated by Christa Unzner-Fischer

Mia the Beach Cat
by Wolfram Hänel, illustrated by Kirsten Höcker

The Old Man and the Bear
by Wolfram Hänel, illustrated by Jean-Pierre Corderoc'h

Lila's Little Dinosaur
by Wolfram Hänel, illustrated by Alex de Wolf

Meet the Molesons
by Burny Bos, illustrated by Hans de Beer